What the Dickens?

Terry Atkinson

Dickens' most popular stories told in rhyme

A note from the author

Charles Dickens is one of the greats in English Literature but, many don't read him beyond school exams because of the often depressing, dark matter, the length of some of his books, the complexity and implausibility of his plots and the use of 19th century English.

This book attempts to address those issues in the form of short(ish), amusing rhymes albeit with occasional modern, juvenile and vulgar terms which, for readers who are unfamiliar with English sayings and colloquialism, are explained in the glossary of terms at the back of the book.

Ten of his most popular works are featured, including his novelette, 'A Christmas Carol'.

The stories are told in the AABB style of rhyme, of varying lengths, depending on the complexity of the tale. Some sub-plots are ignored because they are not vital to the overall story but, in other cases, they would be difficult to ignore.

If the book achieves nothing more than to bring the occasional smile, or equip the reader with a basic knowledge of Dickens' books which they otherwise might not have had, I will have achieved my aim.

All of the lines flow, but it depends how you read them. If you follow the pattern, 'Da-da-da-da-Da-da-da-da-Da-da-da-da-Da', you will not go far wrong. It's a bit of fun. I hope you enjoy it.

CONTENTS

"Please' Sir, I want some more."

OLIVER TWIST

Orphan Ollie, zero lolly, living in a mission,
Asked for more, was shown the door and subbed to a mortician.
When things turned bad, the little lad was turfed out in his slippers,
Walked to the Met, was promptly met by Dodger and some dippers.

Now, Fagin ran the little gang and fenced for Burglar Bill.
Pocket picking was their game, but Ollie wasn't brill.
Within a week he faced the Beak, but due to intervention,
Received a bye from a kind old guy, preventing his detention.

Old Brownlow fed and nurtured him 'til Ollie gained his trust,
Then sent him on an errand but, if only he had sussed
That Fagin's lot were waiting, and to Saffron Hill they took
Poor Ollie and his five-pound note, to resume his trade as crook.

Then Fagin ups the tempo, sending Ollie on a job,
To help Bill burgle fine old kip, to plunder and to rob.
But Ollie makes a hash of things and causes such a clatter,
A servant shoots and captures him, leaving Bill to scatter.

Olly's luck is changing as the old girl takes him in
To dress his wounds and care for him, to get him into trim.
She takes him to the countryside but when he's feeling grand,
He's taken back to London where he's spotted by the band.

"What have paupers to do with soul or spirit? It's quite enough that we left 'em with live bodies. If you had kept that boy on gruel, ma'am, this would never have happened."

When Nancy tells the old girl of Olly's likely plight,
Burglar Bill is livid 'cos he knows he's in the poo.
None too thrilled, wants her killed, so whacks her on the napper,
Opening up her cranium and spilling her grey matter.

The 'hue and cry' goes up and then o'er rooftops they both ran.
Bill slips and falls and hangs himself, which wasn't in his plan.
Then Fagin's caught and dangled, but others dodge the Peelers
And, in time, to resume their crimes as pocket picking stealers.

Then Monks, his brother, different mother, tries to side-line Olly
By destroying proof of bloodline and to pocket all the lolly,
'Cos Ollie's not exactly skint, his dad was rather flush,
But Brownlow learns of Monks's plan and gives the cad the push.

With Ollie's fortunes finally turned, not only has he dosh,
He's living with a family who are really rather posh.
Gent, Brownlow, has adopted him, becomes his loving pater,
And Oliver, now chuffed to bits, lives happily ever after.

The End

"Spirit," said Scrooge with an interest he had never felt before, "Tell me if Tiny Tim will live."

A CHRISTMAS CAROL

Ebenezer, rich old geezer, tight in every way,
Works Bob Cratchit all day long for very little pay.
But Bob has lots of mouths to feed, and life for them is grim,
His youngest, a disabled lad, is known as Tiny Tim.

With Christmas fast approaching, he shuns friends and family
'Til Marley's ghost, who now is toast, calls unexpectedly.
'Scrooge!' he says, 'Mend your ways or end up just like me,
Expect a lecture from a spectre, maybe even three!'

He dozes off and sure enough, just as old Jake had said,
The ghost of 'Christmas Past' arrives and takes him from his bed.
He shows him how life could have been if he was not so greedy.
Girlfriend, family, happy days, being kind towards the needy.

Undaunted, Eb goes back to bed and hides beneath the covers.
'Til 'Christmas Present' leads him off to earwig on his neighbours.
Not a popular man is he, despised, pitied, hated,
But popularity, he feels, is vastly overrated.

And then comes 'Future', number three, the worst one of the lot.
He points to old Eb's tombstone, all neglected and forgot.
The penny drops, Eb sees the light and changes his cruel ways.
Buys Christmas din, saves Tiny Tim and doubles Cratchit's pay.

The End

"Life is made of so many partings welded together."

GREAT EXPECTATIONS

Orphan, Pip, lives in a kip with sis and blacksmith, Joe,
Down by the marsh where life is harsh and few will want to go.
He visits graves of mum and dad and, while in contemplation,
Is jumped by Abel Magwitch, who's escaped his deportation.

He threatens lad with things all bad if he won't bring food and file,
To grind the chains that bind him and to eat, for once, in style.
So, Pip runs off to fetch the scoff and Abel's very glad,
But captors soon catch up with him 'cos he's been rather bad.

Abel takes the rap for Pip, admitting that he stole
The file and grub from blacksmith's house 'cos he was in a hole.
He doesn't want to dob him in, which was against his code, so
He's then dragged back to prison ship a few miles down the road.

Then Pumplechook, Pip's uncle, takes him to a big posh gaff
Where lives rich dame, Miss Haversham, whose life is rather naff.
Jilted at the alter, she still wears her wedding dress,
And even though 'twas years ago, her life is still a mess.

At Satis House, he meets her ward, Estella is her name.
Just as planned, he falls in love, 'twas part of her cruel game.
She groomed the girl to break men's hearts, any male would do,
But Pip was most convenient, it didn't matter who.

"Scattered wits take a long time in picking up."

Pip really thinks the lady wants to raise him as a gent,
To wed him to Estella, a course on which he's bent.
The dowager has other plans, just not what he expected,
She sorts him out a job, alright, Joe Gargery's apprentice!

Mrs Joe, Pip's sister, is attacked and rendered mute
By Orlick, fellow workman, with whom she's in dispute.
Pip knows that he has done it, but evidence is thin,
And Orlick has it on his toes 'cos he knows the fix he's in.

Meantime, Pip's luck changes, with a secret benefactor.
Legal mouthpiece, Jaggers, explains the hereinafter.
He's taken down to London where his life becomes a lark,
With Herbert Pocket and his pop, and Wemmick, Jaggers' clerk.

Then he finds that bad lad, Orlick, now works at Satis House.
He has a word with Jaggers, who tells Haversham he's a louse.
He swears that he'll get even with Pip, the scummy grass,
As once again, the scumbag is turfed out on his bottom.

Years go by, Pip's head is turned and he disowns his folk,
'Til Mrs Joe pops her clogs so, naturally, he's choked.
He knows he's been a plonker, and goes back to the fold,
To visit friends and family, acquaintances of old.

Funeral concluded, he heads back to 'The Smoke'.
Then, one night, and in low light, he's rudely awoke
By convict, Abel Magwitch, who shows up in his room.
He's come back from Australia, having prospered in a boom.

While in Oz, the convict claims, he made it rather rich.
He's Pip's true benefactor, but there's a niggling hitch.
In England, he's a wanted man, he's broken his parole, and
If ever he is captured, they'll *both* be in a hole.

"Take nothing on its looks; take everything on evidence. There is no better rule."

Now, Pip is in a panic, and feeling rather low.
It's not just cops that want this guy, he has *another* foe.
Compeyson, Abel's partner, is baying for his blood,
And sources have detected that he's in the neighbourhood.

So, this is where it twists and turns, you couldn't make it up –
Compeyson's actually Haversham's beau, Estella's Abel's pup.
Regardless of the latest scoop, Pip grows fond of Abel
And vows to help him to escape, as soon as he is able.

He takes time out from planning and to Satis House he trots,
Looking for some answers and to join up all the dots.
He sees the lady and her ward, who now both show remorse
For playing with his feelings, but forgives them both, of course.

He starts off back to London, meantime lady catches fire,
A cinder ignites wedding dress and burns her whole attire.
Regretful though the circumstance, Pip turns his thoughts to Abel,
The means by which he lives in style, has food upon the table.

He also learns Estella is wedded to some bloke,
A rich lout, Bentley Drummle, ending forlorn hope.
Again, he turns to Abel, of whom he's grown to love, and
Escape plan now is ready but it needs help from above.

During preparations for the long-awaited flight,
Orlick, of all people, shows up for a fight.
You couldn't get worse timing and the plan is now delayed,
But Pocket and his pals turn up, save Pip from being flayed.

Orlick does a runner, but things get even worse,
Compeyson, Abel's foe turns up and wants him in a hearse.
Abel is the stronger man and Compeyson is drowned, but
Abel's caught and sentenced, first the hangman then the ground.

"I have been bent and broken, but – I hope – into a better shape."

He's really quite contented, and accepts it's time to go.
He's repaid the lad who helped him, all those years ago.
But what he doesn't know just yet, no matter how hard fought,
His fortune's confiscated, and Pip's now left with nought.

Now, in a depression, Pip becomes quite ill,
And Joe goes down to nurse him, but he can't wait to spill
The beans on badman Orlick, who now is doing bird
For robbing uncle Pumblechook, and being a rotten scamp.

Estella now is taken, and Biddy, second choice,
Has taken up with Gargery, so no time to rejoice.
He goes abroad with Pocket, in whom he had invested
When he had the wherewithal before it was contested.

Years go by and it turns out, Estella's liberated.
Her husband lout had long checked out, so she's no longer gated.
They stay in touch, but in no rush, so don't get too excited,
It may just be platonic, and maybe unrequited.

The End

"The most important thing in life is to stop saying 'I wish and start saying 'I will.' Consider nothing impossible, then treat possibilities as probabilities."

DAVID COPPERFIELD

Dave's dad's dead and mum's re-wed to Murdstone, rich but cruel.
He's brought his sister with him, the household for to rule.
Mum and nice nurse, Peggotty, authority all gone, are
Unable to protect him when he's beaten on the bum.

But Dave is not so helpless, biting bully on the hand,
So off to boarding school he's packed to learn and understand
That biting hand that feeds him, is not a good idea, and
Where strict regime is good for boys, instilling in them, fear.

In happy times, the lad recalls a trip with Peggotty.
To Yarmouth Town in Norfolk, to see her family,
Her brother, also Peggotty, Emily and Ham.
A strapping lad, not much upstairs, but gentle as a lamb.

They live with Mrs Gummidge in a great big upturned boat,
Idyllic setting by the sea, if a tad remote.
Dave takes a shine to Little Em, besotted by her charm,
But all too soon, it's time to go, much to his alarm.

And now, it's time for Salem, run by Creakle, the school head,
Where he meets Steerforth and Traddles, of whom it can be said,
That Tommy Traddles, slightly large, is bullied more than most,
While James Steerforth, an egotist, mostly tends to boast.

"Annual income twenty pounds, annual expenditure, nineteen, nineteen, six, result happiness. Annual income twenty pounds, annual expenditure twenty pounds ought and six, result misery."

But Davey's mum then pops her clogs and, education cut,
Goes home to face the music, but soon he's in a rut, 'cos
Mudstone has sacked Peggotty, and made Dave earn his keep,
In a bottling factory where wages aren't too steep.

He lodges with Micawber, who's financially inept,
Then loses all his money, and finds himself in debt.
Micawber is then rounded up and sent to debtors' nick,
And Davey looks for Aunty Betsey Trotwood and friend, Dick.

A cottage close to Dover, is where he finds the pair.
She's somewhat an eccentric, and nor is *he* all there.
She was present at Dave's birth, after which she took the huff,
She'd really hoped for a little niece, 'cos to her, all boys are duff.

Yet, she takes him in and loves him, and calls him simply, 'Trot',
A shortening of the family name, to him it mattered not.
And for his education, she finds him a new school,
A well-run seat of learning, where self-help is the rule.

While he's there, he lodges with aunt's lawyer and his daughter,
Wickfield and Miss Agnes who, like lambs to the slaughter,
Employ a wily fraudster, whose name's Uriah Heep,
And who claims to be so humble but, he really is a creep.

The fortunes of Miss Trotwood now are sadly on the wane.
Likewise, those of Wickfield, though no one can explain.
But Heep's miscalculated, as Micawber, now his clerk,
Has become highly suspicious, but not yet enough to nark.

And Heep confides in Davey of his fervent wish to wed
The lovely Agnes Wickfield, of whom it must be said,
Is worried 'bout her father as he's wallowing in debt,
And Davey also fancies her but he doesn't know it yet.

"My advice is, never do to-morrow what you can do today. Procrastination is the thief of time. Collar him!"

Dave's now graduated, and off to Yarmouth goes,
To learn that his nurse, Peggotty, has gone and tied the bow
With Barkis, friendly carrier, as they always got on swell, and
It gives them both security, and company as well.

He takes with him James Steerforth, whose friendship he's renewed
And acquaints him with the family, that happy, simple brood.
And good luck or misfortune, we'll have to wait and see,
He gets on well with all of them, *especially* Emily.

Back in London Dave finds work with proctoring in mind,
With Spenlow and friend Jorkins, legal clerking of a kind.
Meanwhile he bumps into friends, Micawber and Traddles, but
Once again, short of dosh, Micawber skedaddles.

Dave falls in love with Dora, but there's an awkward catch,
She's Spenlow's only daughter, he's not keen on the match.
With divine intervention, Spenlow's killed off by a carriage,
Leaving Dave and Dora now available for marriage.

Dave then hears that Barkis is nearing pearly gates,
So, rushes back to Peggotty, to comfort all their mates.
It then transpires that Steerforth and Little Em eloped,
Leaving Ham, her fiancé, and her dad both rightly choked,

Then Betsey's all indignant 'cos her fortune's now all gone.
Embezzled by the rotter, Heep, who's nothing but a con.
Then up steps bold Micawber, who produces Heep's bent books,
And exposes him for what he is, a dirty, rotten crook.

So Wilkins Micawber, hero of the day,
Is rewarded by Aunt Betsey, as she decides to pay
For a ticket and expenses to Oz on board a ship,
For him and all his family, with cash upon the hip.

"It's in vain to recall the past, unless it works some influence on the present."

Hourly expecting that something will transpire,
Micawber's landed on his feet, fulfilling his desire
To ensure that his emoluments exceed his spending rate,
And finally he makes his mark, and becomes a magistrate.

Fortunes are restored, and Heep's now in a cell,
And Dave and Dora marry, but things don't work out well.
'Cos Dora is a sickly girl and housework's not her style
And, during convalescence, shuffles off her mortal coil.

Back in Yarmouth rages a fierce and mighty storm.
A ship is wrecked and locals heed the call, which is the norm.
It's Ham who tries to save a stricken man, but sadly drowns.
Of all people it was Steerforth, the irony abounds.

So, Dave is now a writer, a successful one at that,
He's making lots of money and he knows just where it's at.
He's now in love with Agnes and they marry and have sproggs,
And they all live in comfort, with Betsey, Dick, no dogs.

Meanwhile little Emily is found by brother Dan.
She'd only tried to top herself, as from her life she ran, but
United with her family, they exercise their plan
To emigrate to far-off Oz for Sun, sea and sand.

The End

"Things that are changed or gone will come back as they used to be, thank God! in sleep."

NICHOLAS NICKLEBY

Nick's dad kicks the bucket after losing all his dough.
The family's life in comfort, is history and so,
They shift lodgings to London, moving in with uncle Ralph,
Who takes them in reluctantly and spares the fatted calf.

'Cos Ralph, a money lender, can't abide them, more so Nick, who
Reminds him of his brother, who often gave him stick.
He employs Nick as assistant to the one eyed Wackford Squeers
Who runs a school in Yorkshire for unwanted little dears.

The fees are quite exorbitant but lessons mostly crap,
And Squeers, himself, is clearly an ill-educated chap.
Their parents just want rid of them, they're very rarely missed
And it's likely that not one of them has e're been even kissed.

And Newman Noggs, a businessman, has fallen on hard times,
Now clerks for Ralph, but loathes him, and to Nick he boldly chimes
That if ever Nick should need his help, he'll gladly heed the call,
Ulterior motive being, no doubt, to send Ralph to the wall.

He meets young Smike, an older tyke, who acts as Squeers' runner,
And Fanny, Squeers' daughter, who clearly is no stunner,
Takes a shine to Nicholas, but he is not enthralled,
And he takes evasive action, 'ten-foot bargepole' says it all.

"An elasticity of spirit is happily the lot of young persons, or the world would never be stocked with old ones."

Instead, he fancies Tilda Price who's already engaged.
The lucky man's John Browdie, who is rough but not enraged.
And Fanny has another go, so desperate is she,
The situation's hopeless, so Nick decides to flee.

Squeers is now enraged by his daughter's cruel rebuff,
And takes to beating Nick's new friend, Smike, for whom it's tough.
But Nick comes to the rescue, beating Squeers until he's sore,
And when his daughter intervenes, he beats her dad some more.

He meets John Browdie as he leaves, who thinks it's rather funny,
And Browdie gladly gives Nick help with a walking stick and money.
It's a long way back to London, and he's grateful for assistance,
Especially when Smike turns up and stays with him the distance.

Meanwhile, back in London, mum and sis live in a dump.
Their lodgings now downgraded, as Ralph still has the hump.
Apprenticed to a milliner, sister Kate will get to sew
With Madame Mantalini and her husband gigolo.

Her boss, Knag, is delighted when her work is not spot on,
She'll make an ideal scapegoat, if ever things go wrong.
But when a client asks for Kate, preferring her to Knag,
The girls all turn against her, 'cos they fear more the old bag.

Noggs now has the letter that Fanny Squeers penned
To Ralph about the beating of her dad, who's on the mend.
When Nick goes to confront his uncle, Ralph is out of town,
So, he tries to find employment but, nothing's going down.

Ralph then gives a dinner, inviting business mates.
Kate's invited, only girl, it's obvious she's bait
To entice Lord Fred Verisopht, a gullible rich dude,
But Mulberry Hawk, spoils it all by being rather crude.

"Happiness is a gift and the trick is not to expect it, but to delight in it when it comes."

He's made a bet at Kate's expense, and she's now in a muddle,
She flees the room, indignant, then Hawk gives her a cuddle.
Then Ralph comes to the rescue but persuades her to keep shtum,
Or else he'll pull the help he gives to Kate and her old mum.

Then Nick finds out his unc is back and visits mum and Kate.
Ralph is reading them Squeers note, which really isn't great.
Clearly there's still no love lost 'tween Ralph and his nephew.
He threatens that if Nick stays on, then both the girls are through.

So, Nick and Smike leave London, and off to Portsmouth go,
To join low-grade theatricals, and take part in a show.
His Romeo is well received but, elsewhere, miles from here,
Mantalini's firm goes bust and Kate's out on her ear.

Then Kate becomes companion to Mrs Wititterly,
While Hawk, who's still annoyed with Kate, is plotting dastardly.
With Verisopht, he goes to Ralph to ask where Kate resides, but
Unknowing, mother spills the beans, the low, conniving snides.

Wititterly is jealous of the fuss they make of Kate.
Accusing her of flirting, she could not anticipate, that
Kate would jump right down her throat and give her boss what for,
The consequence of which would be her showing to the door.

Kate is now in dire straits but Ralph won't intervene,
'Cos Verisopht and Hawk are mates and he won't dob them in.
So, Noggs writes to her brother, Nick, who rises to the bait,
By giving up his thespian chums to concentrate on Kate.

Intent on writing wrongs for Kate, Nick searches for the creeps.
He finds them in a coffee house, bragging of their feats.
Escaping in his carriage, Hawk delivers Nick some lashes, so
Nick hits back and, horses spooked, the carriage goes and crashes.

"The pain of parting is nothing to the joy of meeting again."

Intent on retribution, Hawk then issues Nick a threat, but
Lord Verisopht, who now sees sense, opposes Hawk and lets
Hawk know of his displeasure, and dumps him on his pants.
A duel is billed, Verisopht's killed and Hawk does off to France.

Nick then writes to his uncle, severing all his ties,
And takes up with the Cheerybles, benevolent rich guys.
They give him house and salary, a merchant he becomes, and
His mum and Kate now have a roof, so goodbye to the slums.

Ralph chances on a beggar who was once in his employ,
He says he has a secret, that Ralph would not enjoy.
Ralph won't give in to blackmail so, he drives the man away,
Then goes home to Nick's letter, which brightens up his day.

Ralph then uses Wackford Squeers to kidnap Smike, Nick's friend,
But Browdie sees what's going down, and he decides to lend
A hand to rescue hapless Smike, while he and Squeers eat.
And when the time is right, the pair leg it down the street.

Then Ralph and Squeers, undeterred, hatch another plan,
To forge parental papers showing Smike's dad's back in town.
They deliver the said forgery at a party held by Nick,
To say thank you to Browdie, for pulling off his trick.

Smike is far from happy and is disinclined to go.
Meantime, Nick bumps into the chick he first saw at the dole.
The daughter of Ralph's debtor, and her name is Maddie Bray, who
Survives on Cheerybles' charity, 'cos she can't live on hay.

Arthur Gride, a miser, who's aware that when she weds,
She'll inherit a small fortune from her grandpa, who's now dead.
So, he and Ralph persuade her dad to let his girl get hitched
To Gride, with the incentive that his debt to Ralph is ditched.

"To remember happiness which cannot be restored, is pain, but of a softened kind."

Reluctantly, Bray does agree, the news reaches Nick's ear.
He's fallen for the girl, himself, so he gets his bum in gear
To stymie the arrangements, but in the nick of time,
Maddie's daddy dies, so he no longer owes a dime.

So, no need for the wedding, Nick and Kate then rescue Maddie,
And Gride finds that his housekeeper has turns into a baddy.
She stole Maddie's grandpa's will, the one that Gride had pinched
To discover her inheritance, for which he could be lynched.

To get it back, he hires Squeers to find out where she's gone,
But Noggs beats Squeers to it, as he knows what's going on.
The Will is now recovered and the evidence secure,
Then Squeers is locked up, bang to rights, Australia for sure.

Meanwhile, Smike is gravely ill with TB, soon to croak, and
On his death bed he points out the man, a shifty bloke,
Who took him to Squeers' awful school, where he felt quite bereft,
But before he can do much about it, draws his final breath.

Squeers decides to cough the lot and Ralph's future is sealed,
But Ralph decides to tough it out, then Smike's fate is revealed.
He's delighted at the outcome, that Nick's friend has clocked out,
'Til Brooker, beggar, ex-employee, again pokes in his snout.

The kid Ralph had with former wife, before they parted ways,
Had not died, of that he'd lied, instead he'd spent his days
At Squeers's school for waifs and strays, unwanted little tykes,
The name of which he'd know him by, is the dear departed Smike.

Ralph is now beside himself on learning what he's done,
No peace for him who celebrates the death of his own son.
He takes a rope and hangs himself and he dies intestate.
No claimants for his fortune so, his wealth goes to the State.

"Now. Now I can say it. I am happy."

So, just as was expected, Squeers is sent to Oz,
Browdie helps Squeers' boys escape and all goes well for Noggs.
Nick and Maddie wed and live in Devon by the sea,
And despite their past encumbrances, they all live happily.

The End

"You might, from your appearance, be the wife of Lucifer," said Miss Pross, in her breathing. "Nevertheless, you shall not get the better of me. I am an Englishwoman."

A TALE OF TWO CITIES

Manette, kind doctor, slightly mad from years in Bastille nick,
To England goes to live with daughter, Lucie, who's a chick.
She marries an aristocrat from France, who's on the rack
Because his head is for the chop if ever he goes back.

Charles Darnay is the lucky man, but he could well still die,
As, back in England, he's on trial for treason, as a spy.
But lawyer, Sidney Carton, gets him off quite cleverly,
'Cos he looks just like his client, casting doubt on his i.d.

Then Darnay, who's foolhardy, takes a reckless chance.
Missing all his relatives, he heads off back to France
Where revolution's in full swing, he's spotted and locked up.
His head is coming off for sure, unless he has some luck.

His real name is St. Evremonde, a name he had to drop
'Cos his family are aristocrats and they're all for the chop.
His uncle, Marquis, killed a child, and then he callously
Threw a coin at the dead kid's dad for the undertaker's fee.

The dead kid's father later stabs the Marquis in his bed.
Rebellion then intensifies, and many, now, are dead.
'Twas open season on the nobs and heads rolled by the score,
And Darnay's would be one of them, if they had their way, for sure.

"It is a far, far better thing that I do, than I have ever done; it is a far, far better rest that I go to, than I have ever known."

Manette and his daughter try to reason with the court.
Success at first but thwarted, as new evidence is brought.
Tomorrow, now, is his last day, the dreaded final phase
Before his head and body suffer parting of the ways.

Meanwhile, Carton, who's in love with Lucie, Darnay's wife,
Volunteers to take his place and forfeit his own life.
He's been a disappointment, and he'd like to make amends,
If he could do this one good deed, he'd make posthumous friends.

So, Carton then mans up and visits Darnay in his cell.
He drugs him and exchanges clothes, the cunning plan goes well.
Darnay's taken back to Blighty, Carton now will dread,
For he'll soon meet Madame Guillotine, in Darnay's place instead.

Defarge and other rebels, aware of Lucie's plan,
Chase after her and daughter, to catch them if they can.
Lucie's maid, Miss Pross, steps in and tussles with their head.
A gun goes off, the rebel drops, Defarge is now brown bread.

No greater love can there be than a man who gives his life
For the sake of someone's happiness, especially someone's wife.
'Tis a far, far better thing he's done, than he has done before,
And very soon his severed head will be rolling on the floor.

The End

"No one is useless in this world who lightens the burdens of another."

OUR MUTUAL FRIEND

Old skinflint, Mr Harmon, dies, the only heir, his son,
Who's been abroad these last few years and is due a hefty sum
Of money, if he marries Bella Wilfer, local lass,
But he knows nothing of her, so his dad's been rather crass.

As it happens, she's a looker, but John Harmon won't find out,
'Cos his body's in the river, Gaffer Hexam pulled it out.
The money now will go to Noddy Boffin and his wife,
Employees of old Harmon and who've led a sheltered life.

The pair take in Miss Bella and her fortunes now have turned,
If she had wed young Harmon, she'd have money, now, to burn,
Instead, she'll have to settle for the generosity
Of the Boffins, who will come to treat her as their heir to be.

In a quest to be accepted by polite society,
Boffin hires a ballad reader, Silas Wegg, for a small fee,
He reads to them some stories so that they are in the know,
'Cos, back then there was no telly and no wireless radio.

A fellow called John Rokesmith rents some rooms from Bella's dad.
He was present when John's body was identified, but had
Given police a pseudonym instead of his real name, now
He's wanted by the cops, who still don't know who is to blame.

"Have a heart that never hardens, and a temper that never tires, and a touch that never hurts."

The death is quite suspicious, could be murder, in their book,
But they have such little evidence and don't know where to look.
If Handford, the false name he gave, came forward and explained,
They could file the case as 'sorted' and no one would be detained.

It helps that Noddy Boffin now has offered a reward
For information leading to a suspect being caught.
The generous and vastly sum, tempts Roger Riderhood,
Hexam's dodgy partner, who is up to no real good.

Meanwhile Rokesmith worms his way into the Boffin's modest pad,
He's now the secretary of old Boffin, who is glad
To give this educated chap the chance to do his thing,
While enjoying all the benefits themselves, the fellow brings.

But Rokesmith, alias Handford, who isn't who he said,
Is actually young John Harmon and he's far from being dead.
He knows full well what's in the will, 'marry or take flight',
So, he watches Bella closely to assess whether he might.

He sees that she's ambitious, her priorities quite sad, and
Boffin is mistaken 'bout the prospects of the lad.
He thinks of him a fortune hunter, looking to make good
At his and her expense and so, to the lad he's rude.

But Boffin and his missus are part of young John's game
To see if Bella likes the lad, more than cash and fame.
When they realised who he was, they all hatched a plot, and
When the time was right for her, they'd reveal to her the lot.

Meanwhile, she is mellowing and slowly comes to suss
That wealth is superficial and no substitute for trust.
She leaves her home for Rokesmith who, to all intents, is poor,
And yet she marries him not knowing who he is, for sure.

"No one who can read, ever looks at a book, even unopened on a shelf, like one who cannot."

Elsewhere, Hexam doesn't know he's suspect number one,
'Cos Riderhood has told the cops that he is on the run
For Harmon's callous killing, but by chance *his* body's found
Face down in the river, by coincidence he's *drowned.*

Meanwhile Charley Hexam's son who's bright, now goes to school,
His ambition is to be a teacher 'cos he's no one's fool.
While Eugene Wrayburn, barrister, is keen on Charley's sis,
But Lizzie's from a lower class so his friends will take the micky.

But Charley's teacher, Bradley Headstone's fallen for the same
Lizzie Hexam, who is lush, so he should not be blamed.
And, jealous of the barrister, he beats him 'round the head,
Then dumps him in the river, and leaves the man for dead.

It's Lizzie who then rescues him and pulls the fellow out.
She's fallen deeply for the man, of that there is no doubt.
They marry on his sickbed and although he's feeling rough,
They will not prosecute the man 'cos to lose Liz is enough.

But Riderhood has evidence that Headstone's been a fool, and
Blackmails the schoolmaster in front of his own school.
Since Headstone has no money, he decides to take him down, and
When they fall into the river, both of them are drowned.

Then Silas Wegg, the ballad man, soon turns into a lout,
He finds a will of Harmon that post-dates the one read out.
It leaves the whole lot to the State, sole beneficiary, and
He's willing to keep schtum about it, for a hefty fee.

But Boffin and his missus both know about the plot, 'cos
Mr Venus spilled the beans and now they know the lot.
Allowing him to show his hand and get right down to biz,
They then produce another will post-dating even his.

"Give me a moment, because I like to cry for joy. It's so delicious, John dear, to cry for joy."

This one leaves the lot to them and nothing to young John,
But their sense of fair play sees them make a new will of their own.
They'll take care of the money, but when their lives are through,
They'll leave it to the couple so that they'll enjoy it too.

Then, the police catch up with Harmon, who explains the mystery,
The drowned man was a lookalike pretending to be he, while
The decoy was distracting folk, John hoped he'd get the chance
To assess his father's nominee and maybe find romance.

But before the plan was activated, both were set about,
Then dumped into the river, but only John climbed out.
The other was recovered, to the morgue went his remains,
And the rest of it is history, foregoing tale explains.

The End

"In the majority of cases, conscience is an elastic and very flexible article."

THE OLD CURIOSITY SHOP

Little Nell, aged thirteen, lives with grandpa in his shop,
Selling curiosities and cleaning out his slop.
She also has a brother, Fred, who lives elsewhere in town,
A waster with no income, lack of money gets him down.

He won't believe that grandpa isn't hiding all his wealth, and
Swiveller, tries to court young Nell and find his stash by stealth.
But grandpa's really stony broke and he's in lots of debt,
He lost it all by playing cards, much to his regret.

His ambition was to set Nell up, a lady with fine gowns, but
His weakness left him potless, now, he must get out of town.
He has a loan shark after him, Dan Quilp, an evil dwarf
Who lives in a fine townhouse, with an office by the wharf.

Quilp is rather sweet on Nell but the feeling's not returned.
He's angry and rejected, and feeling rather spurned.
He forecloses on her grandpa's loan, an act of pure spite, so
Grandpa does a flit with Nell, leaving through the night.

Young Kit, their shop assistant, who now is unemployed,
Finds work with the Garlands, so he is overjoyed.
He then meets with a gentleman, who will not give his name,
He's the brother of Nell's grandpa, and they share a common aim.

"Women don't always tell the truth about their age."

But Quilp is likewise on the trail, helped by a shady snout.
Meantime, Nell, who's put to work, is weary and worn out.
She's had jobs at a waxwork theatre and a travelling fair,
While grandpa's unaware she's ailing 'cos *he's not all there.*

Quilp forces Brass, his legal ass, to take on Swiveller
To keep an eye upon the guy, as he may lead him to her.
He also wants revenge on Kit, as the two don't get along,
And uses Brass to fit him up, but the lad has done no wrong.

A banknote has been planted in his cap, and he is caught,
By a cop who likely knew the score, but still took him to court.
Then Swiveller and the 'marchioness', pet name of Brass's maid,
Step up with the evidence that the whole thing had been staged.

Brass panics, turns Queen's evidence and dobs Quilp in for lots,
And it's likely he will hang or stay inside until he rots.
The bad news reaches Quilps's ears, he reaches for his coat,
And gathers his ill-gotten gains and then, unties his boat.

He falls into the water but, unable to climb out,
The coins and jewels weigh him down, so he hasn't got a shout.
He's dragged down to the muddy depths, a fate he well deserves,
But his wife will soon get over it 'cos he got on her nerves.

With Quilp now gone, the race is on to find grandpa and Nell.
They find them but she's passed away, 'cos she has not been well.
Her journey had been long and hard, she'd caught a nasty cough,
She was caught out in a downpour, now, the fever's seen her off.

Grandpa's feeling guilty as he knows he is to blame,
He's pushed her hard to earn some dosh, to stake him in a game.
And its likely that his grandson, Fred's now in a debtors' cell,
But as far as grandpa is concerned, the lad can go to France.

"Have I yet to learn that the hardest and best-borne trials are those which are never chronicled in any earthly record, and are suffered every day."

And though his long-lost brother's home, there is no help for him,
He's brought his guilt upon himself, there's no one else to blame.
He was sitting pretty for a time, until he became hooked,
Then he threw it all away with gambling, now his goose is cooked.

The End

"There are times when ignorance is bliss indeed."

THE PICKWICK PAPERS

Pickwick, a retiree, who is jolly, rich and kind
Starts a club for gentlemen, to study all mankind.
Including him they number four and they all have their querks,
Tupman, Snodgrass, Winkle who, it must be said, are jerks.

Tupman's a lothario, but rarely gets a bird.
Snodgrass is a poet but, he hardly writes a word,
Winkle claims he's sporty but, he's naff at everything,
Their adventures, quite predictably, will not go with a swing.

On their very first assignment, Pickwick gets into a fight
With a coachman who accuses him, suspecting that he might
Be a busybody, asking questions, writing notes,
'Til conman, Jingle, intervenes and takes them by their coats.

He takes them to their hostelry and joins them all for scoff.
They all get drunk, three fall asleep while Tups and he slope off
To a charity event upstairs, where they can have some fun,
But Jingle causes mayhem and the pair then have to run.

Slammer, the aggrieved man, wants to duel the pushy bloke, who
He's wrongly identified as Winkle, by his coat.
'Cos Jingle borrowed Winkle's coat while he was fast asleep,
And Winkle now is in the clarts, he'll soon his maker meet.

"Great men are seldom overscrupulous in the arrangement of their attire."

But when the two line up to shoot, the danger soon abates,
As Slammer sees the error so, they head home with their mates.
Winkle then investigates what led to his close shave,
And comes to the conclusion that Jingle is a knave.

They then move on to Chatham, to watch the army play,
Then Wardle, county squire, invites them home to stay.
They head for lovely Dingley Dell, but horses then play up,
And they end up walking to the house, where they can't get enough.

There are women, games and hunting, but soon they're in the mire,
'Cos Tupman falls for Rachael, younger sister of the squire.
She's plain and really desperate, gullible and dim, and
When Jingle makes a better offer, Rachael goes with him.

He tells her that friend, Tupman, is fake and insincere,
He's really talking 'bout himself, but now he has her ear.
He takes her down to London, with the licence in his mitt.
He'll ditch her once he's cleaned her out, 'cos he's a little rascal.

Pickwick, who's indignant heads to London with the toff.
They're just in time to bribe him, and then he beetles off.
He comes across Sam Weller, who's a shoe cleaner by trade,
And hires him as his valet, now, the fellow's got it made.

Then Pickwick tells his landlady he's taken on a man.
His explanation is misleading, so she misunderstands.
She thinks that he's proposing and she swoons into his arms,
As witnessed by his comrades who, bewildered, are alarmed.

Meanwhile, Pickwick and his members go to Eatanswill to stay
With Mr Potts, an editor, who's having a bad day.
They witness an election where they've broken all the rules, and
They come to the conclusion that the place is run by fools.

"I wants to make your flesh creep."

They're invited to a literary breakfast by some loon,
Mrs Leo Hunter, whose shenanigans will soon
Lead to introductions they'd be better to avoid, and
When Jingle shows up suddenly, the host is overjoyed.

This time, Jingle's posing as a famous pioneer,
He calls himself Fitz-Marshall, explorer, mountaineer.
He knows that he's now rumbled so he beats a quick retreat
To a pub in London so that he can dodge the heat.

His accomplice, who is posing as his manservant, is there.
He strikes a deal with Weller, who thinks he is sincere, but
He's just another conman, who is cooking up a plan
To embarrass Mr Pickwick, and to buy time for his man.

He claims Captain Fitz-Marshall is going to elope
With a lady from a school for girls, and very much he'd hope
That Pickwick would then intervene and catch them as they leave,
But he soon finds out he's been set up, and cleverly deceived.

When the plan to expose Jingle doesn't work out, he is left
To explain it to the ladies, who are worried and perplexed.
They send out for a magistrate, but they have met before
At Leo Hunter's breakfast bash so, vouched for, he can go.

As was anticipated, Mr Pickwick's in a fix.
Landlady, Mrs Bartell's briefs are now up to their tricks.
They'll file a breach of promise writ unless he shows remorse,
But Pickwick will contest it, 'cos he's innocent, of course.

He then learns Mr Jingle is in Ipswich on a quest
To woo a rich young lady but, he'll try to do his best
To warn the lady off him, as he's dodgy as they come,
So, he finds an inn in Ipswich where he'll stay until it's done.

"Poetry makes life what lights and music do the stage."

He goes to the wrong bedroom, and a lady's compromised.
The matter's taken to the bench where he is ostracised.
The magistrate's the father of the girl in Jingle's thoughts, and
When Pickwick warns dad of the plan, he then is freed from court.

Then Pickwick and his members, are all feeling rather smug,
They spend Christmas at the Wardle's farm, partaking of their grub.
They're present at the wedding of their daughter Isabella,
And Winkle falls for her good friend, the lovely Arabella.

The day of reckoning arrives, on Valentine's Day.
A guilty verdict is returned and Pickwick has to pay
A sum of money to Bardell, and Fogg and Dodson's fees,
But he declines to pay the briefs, because he disagrees.

He's quite prepared to go to prison, just to make his point.
It's not what he'd expected, it's a soul-destroying joint.
His valet, Weller, joins him just to give him company, and
They pay a bribe for a separate room, to give them privacy.

Then purely by coincidence, Jingle's there as well.
The law has since caught up with him, and now he's just a shell.
But Pickwick, a true gentleman, takes pity on his woes, and
Gives him enough money to buy food and nicer clothes.

And Mrs Bardell joins them, even *she* can't pay her debt
To Fogg and Dodson, law firm, who want their pound of flesh.
Pickwick to the rescue, relents and comes about,
He clears her debt as well as his, then everyone's let out.

Winkle weds his lady, comrades wish him all the best, and
Pickwick, full of energy, declines the chance to rest.
He'll continue to explore the country, breadth and end to end,
Enhancing his experience and sharing it with friends.

The End

"It is a melancholy truth that even great men have their poor relations."

BLEAK HOUSE

Sir Lester Dedlock and his wife live in Chesney Wold,
She's connected to a legacy, but there's a very old
Court case that's been going on 'cos no one can agree,
Jarndyce and Jarndyce, concerning family.

There are several conflicting wills and the court is in a spin,
Deciding who gets what from whom, who's out and who is in.
It seems like orphan, Ada Clare, and orphan, Rick Carstone,
Are the favourites to benefit, and they now have a home.

The judge decrees they are to live with John Jarndyce, their cuz,
Who lives in Bleak House on his own, so now he gets a buzz
From having such good company, a companion, to boot,
To fill the hours until the court can finalise the suit.

Then Tulkinghorn, a lawyer, calls at Dedlock's house to read
Some papers appertaining to the case his wife must heed.
Honoria, seeing the style in which an affidavit's penned,
Takes a wobbler, faints and brings proceedings to an end.

The silk suspects there's maybe more to this than meets the eye,
Perhaps she's been a naughty girl with a secret to deny.
He finds out who the author is, Nemo, local scribe,
But when he calls at Nemo's room, the poor chap's gone and died.

"The children of the very poor are not brought up, but dragged up."

We know he's educated 'cos his writing's very grand,
But he can't afford to pay his rent 'though his skill is in demand.
He's also been a soldier but he's had to sell his gongs,
It's a mystery where his money goes, so something's very wrong.

The word is, he liked opium, Honoria liked rich dudes,
They're really Esther's mum and dad and haven't heard the news
That Esther's very much alive, a new life she has found, but
It's already too late for him, he's six feet underground.

Little Jo, an urchin, knew the mystery man quite well,
And Lady Honoria found and begged the lad to tell
Her where the body's buried so that she can go and bid
Farewell to Captain 'Nemo' Hawdon, father of her kid.

To do it incognito, she dresses as her maid,
A French mamzel called Hortense, of whom it should be said
Doesn't like her boss a lot, 'cos she has been replaced
By a younger model, Rosa, leaving her disgraced.

She knows that Tulkinghorn suspects, and wants to help him out
By telling him of what she knows, and hopes he'll bring about
Her exposure and her fall from grace, pay-back for the sleight,
But Tulkinghorn just sits on it, until the time is right.

He also tells maid, Hortense, that he'll help her find a job,
He's grateful for the help she gave, so he owes her a few bob.
Then Guppy, who's a lawyer's clerk, finds the missing link,
Esther's real name's Hawdon, and it's bound to raise a stink.

Tulkinghorn then tells the lady what he has found out, and
Assures her that his lips are sealed, but then he turns about.
'Cos, fuming at her change of staff and feigning that he's hurt,
He leaves it hanging in the air, not saying if he'll blurt.

"All partings foreshadow the great final one."

Honoria knows the score on Nemo, she and Esther meet.
She tells her of her birthright, and hopes she'll be discreet.
But Esther blabs to Jarndyce as the pair see eye to eye, and
He proposes that they wed so she can hold her head up high.

Tulkinghorn's now reeling and decides he's going to tell
Sir Leicester of the scandal, 'cos there'll be merry Hell, but
Before he gets to blab the lot, his body's found shot dead,
'Cos Hortense, who was feeling used, has filled him full of lead.

She blames it on the lady, sending cops accusing notes, but
Inspector Bucket, in good time, will see through what she wrote.
But then a handy suspect walks right into the frame,
Rouncewell, Dedlock's housemaid's son who's really not to blame.

Meanwhile, Carstone's looking for a job, but there's a tricky glitch,
He'd rather sit it out until the court case makes him rich.
He starts by learning medicine, army and the law, but
His heart is not in any, 'cos he's lazy to the core.

Then Bucket tells Sir Leicester of his lawyer's sad demise,
Including what's behind it all, what problems may arise.
His lady is a suspect, but then so are other folk, and
Sir Leicester takes it badly, and goes and has a stroke.

He forgives his wife's misconduct, he has some sympathy,
While the spotlight's now on Hortense, meaning others can go free.
It's too late for her ladyship, who wanders in disgrace, and
Her body's found on snowy ground, outside the graveyard gates.

Her heart is clearly broken, her life has been a lie,
She gave up love and motherhood for a bigger piece of pie,
Unlike Carstone and Ada Clare who, penniless, still wed,
Hoping that the Jarndyce case will soon be put to bed.

"The legal profession, where writs are issued, judgements signed, declarations filed, and numerous other ingenious little machines put in motion for the torture and torment of His Majesty's liege subjects, and the comfort and emolument of the practitioners of the law."

Meantime, Jo's caught smallpox, and Esther, just the same.
The young lad dies, Esther survives, but her boat-race is a shame.
And Woodcourt, the physician, to young Rick while he was ill,
Despite her spots, has got the hots for Esther, who is brill.

His love's reciprocated but she's spoken for by John.
She tells him and he understands, he knows his love's forlorn.
He gives them both his blessing and they marry and have kids.
Meanwhile, hope is fading for the wards, the case is on the skids.

For all it's going to Carstone, the fortune's now all gone,
The lawyers have all seen to that, their fees all weigh a ton.
And Ricky-boy can't handle it, he falls ill then he dies,
His eggs were in one basket, instead of many pies.

The End

Glossary of Terms

Term	Meaning
Ass	Bottom, backside, fool, work-horse
Bargepole (10')	Uncomplimentary, long pole to keep a person at a desirable distance
Beak	Magistrate
Beau	Boyfriend, fiance
Bent	Fraudulent
Bigger piece of pie	Wanted more, a bigger share
Blab	Tell, inform
Blighty	England
Bloke	Man
Blurt	Tell, inform
Boat race	Cockney rhyming slang for 'face'
Boot (to)	In addition
Brief	Solicitor, lawyer
Brown bread	Dead
Brill	Brilliant, good
Bum	Bottom, backside
Cad	Untrustworthy, unpleasant person
Checked out	Died
Chick	Attractive girl
Chimes	Says, announces
Choked	Annoyed, regretful
Chuffed to bits	Really pleased, happy
Clarts	Trouble, mud
Clocks/clocked out	Dies, died
Comes about	Changes mind, makes a u-turn
Con	Criminal, confidence trickster
'Cos	Because
Crap	Abuse, rubbish
Croak	Die
Cuz	Cousin

Dangled	Hanged
Dears	Lovable people
Deportation	In Britain, during the 19th century, convicts were often sent to Australia to work, but if they returned home, they risked being hanged.
Din	Dinner
Dippers	Pick-pockets
Ditched	Forgotten about, negated
Dob in	Implicate, inform on someone
Does off	Leaves in a hurry
Dole	Labour/employment exchange,
Dosh	Money
Dough	Money
Duff	Rubbish, unserviceable
Dump	Slum
Dumps him on his pants	Knocks him down (metaphorically speaking)
Earwig	Listen
Eggs in one basket instead of many pies	Risk is all in one place instead of spreading the risk to minimise loss.
Fenced	Handle stolen goods
Few bob	Money – an old English shilling was called a 'bob'
Fit him up	Produce/manufacture false evidence
Fix (a)	Quandary, state of confusion
Flush	Wealthy
Gaff	House
Gated	Kept indoors
Gave him stick	Annoyed him, gave him abuse
Geezer	Man
Give her boss what for	Tell her boss off
Gongs	Medals
Goose is cooked	Wrongdoing has been discovered and there's

	no going back
Grass	Informant
Grey matter	Brains
Grub	Food
Has her ear	She will readily listen to him
He's not all there	Mentally deficient
Hitched	Married
Hole	Trouble
Hue and cry	Old English term mean raising the alarm and giving chase
Huff	Annoyed, strop
Hump	Annoyed, strop
i.d.	Identification
Jerk	Fool
Jumped	Pounced upon
Jump right down her throat	Be bad tempered
Kicks the bucket	Dies
Kip	House
Knave	Dishonest, unscrupulous man
Lark	Laugh, enjoyable
Leg it	Run away
Lolly	Money
Loon	Lunatic, eccentric person
Mamzel	Mademoiselle (unmarried French lady)
Mans up	Becomes bold, manly
Met	The metropolitan district of London
Mitt	Hand
Mouthpiece	Solicitor, lawyer
Naff	Not good, rubbish
Napper	Head
Nob	Member of the nobility
Not much upstairs	Not very bright

Nought	Nothing, zero
O'er	Old English – short for 'over'
Old bag	Old lady (derogatory)
Old doll	Old lady (neutral as regards appearance)
On her ear	Dismissed
Oz	Australia
Parting of the ways	XXXeparated, severed
Pater	Father (Latin)
Pearly gates	The entrance to Heaven
Peelers	Policemen, so named after the prime minister Robert Peel who created the first British police force in 1829
Planted	Put there so that it would be found
Plonker	Fool, silly person
Pop	Father, dad
Pops clogs	Dies
Potless	Without money
Pound of flesh	Payment in full
Pup	Child
Push (the)	The sack, dismissed
Put to bed	Finalised
Queens evidence	Guilty party who gives evidence against an accomplice in return for clemency or partial clemency
Rumbled	Found out
Scoff	Food
Schtum	Quiet
Scribe	Writer
Seen her off	Killed her
Shell	Empty, shadow of his former self
Shout (hasn't got a)	Hasn't got a chance
Showing to the door	The sack, dismissal
Shuffles off her mortal coil	Dies
Sis	Sister

Skedaddles	Leaves, runs off
Skids	In jeopardy
Skint	Short of money
Slope off	Sneak away
Smoke (The)	London (nickname)
Snide	Sneaky person
Snout (sticks in)	Interrupts, intervenes
Spares fatted calf	Does little to celebrate
Spill the beans	Inform on, tell a secret
Spin (in a)	Undecided
Spot on	Exact
Sproggs	Children
Stash	Money or goods hidden away
Stony broke	Without money
Stunner	Attractive lady
Subbed	Loaned, contracted to
Suit	Court case
Sussed	Suspected
Tad	Little
Tight	Thrifty, selfish
'Til	Old English, short for 'until'
Toast	Dead
Toes (on his)	Runs away
Top herself	Kill herself
'Twas	Old English, short for 'it was'
'Tween	Old English, short for 'between'
Tyke	Young person, tearaway
Unc	Uncle
Ward	Person for whom parental responsibility or guardianship is awarded by a court
Wobbler (takes a)	Momentary unsteadiness